ROAD
BUILDERS

BY B. G. HENNESSY · PICTURES BY SIMMS TABACK

PUFFIN BOOKS

The artwork was done using
pen and ink, airbrush, and
cut Cello-Tak color sheets.

PUFFIN BOOKS
Published by the Penguin Group
Penguin Books USA Inc., 375 Hudson Street, New York, New York 10014, U.S.A.
Penguin Books Ltd, 27 Wrights Lane, London W8 5TZ, England
Penguin Books Australia Ltd, Ringwood, Victoria, Australia
Penguin Books Canada Ltd, 10 Alcorn Avenue, Toronto, Ontario, Canada M4V 3B2
Penguin Books (N.Z.) Ltd, 182-190 Wairau Road, Auckland 10, New Zealand
Penguin Books Ltd, Registered Offices: Harmondsworth, Middlesex, England

First published in the United States of America by Viking,
a division of Penguin Books USA Inc., 1994
Published in Puffin Books, 1996

43

THE LIBRARY OF CONGRESS HAS CATALOGED THE VIKING EDITION AS FOLLOWS:
Hennessy, B. G. (Barbara G.)
Road builders / B. G. Hennessy ; illustrated by Simms Taback.   p.   cm.
1. Road machinery—Juvenile literature. 2. Roads—Design and construction—Juvenile literature.
[1. Roads—Design and construction. 2. Road machinery.] I. Taback, Simms, ill. II. Title.
TE223.H43   1994   625.7—dc20   93-42248

Puffin Books ISBN 978-0-14-054276-9

Printed in the United States of America
Set in Futura Medium Condensed

To my favorite road builders:
Matt, Mark, and Brett

—B. G. H.

To Sean and to Jay Baugher

—S. T.

It takes many kinds of trucks to build a road.

Pickup trucks, cement mixers, bulldozers, dump trucks, backhoes, graders, crane trucks,

power shovels, front loaders, pavers, power rollers, striper trucks, and cherry-picker trucks.

Here are Buddy, John, Ed, Fran, Joe, Jessie, and Chuck.
They are going to build a road.

Buddy is the boss. He follows a plan
that shows where the road is going to be
and tells everyone what to do.

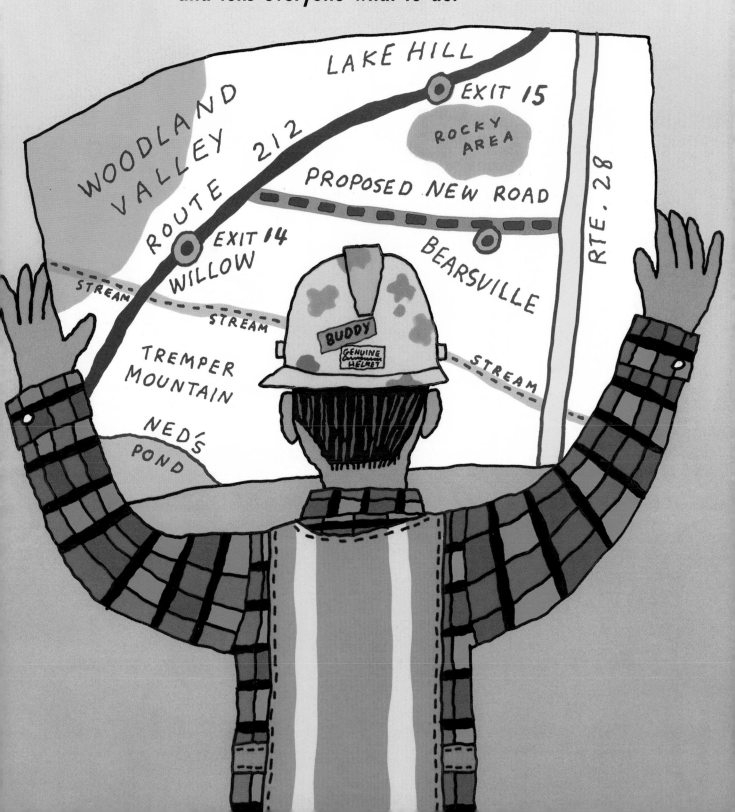

The power shovel scoops and lifts the dirt.

A bulldozer pushes the dirt away.

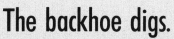

The backhoe digs.

The front loader pushes and carries dirt and rocks,

which the dump trucks carry away.

The grader smooths the ground.

Dump trucks bring in gravel for the roadbed.
A cement mixer pours cement down a chute
to make the gutters at the sides of the road.

Then dump trucks dump asphalt into
the paver truck. Asphalt is a mixture
of stones, stone dust, and gooey tar.
The paver lays the asphalt on the roadbed.

The power roller packs it down
so that the road is smooth.

A truck called a striper paints the lines on the center of the road.

The crane truck raises a sign.

The cherry-picker truck lifts a worker, who puts up the lights.

At last the road is finished.
The road builders are gone.
Now the road is ready.

And here come moving vans, taxicabs,
delivery trucks, motorcycles, school buses, RVs . . .

... family cars, fire engines, horse trailers,

soda-bottle trucks, police cars, jeeps, sports cars . . .

. . . and flatbed trucks
carrying the road builders
to their next job.